Dear Parents and Educators,

Welcome to Penguin Young Readers! As parents and educators, you know that each child develops at his or her own pace—in terms of speech, critical thinking, and, of course, reading. Penguin Young Readers recognizes this fact. As a result, each Penguin Young Readers book is assigned a traditional easy-to-read level (1–4) as well as a Guided Reading Level (A–P). Both of these systems will help you choose the right book for your child. Please refer to the back of each book for specific leveling information. Penguin Young Readers features esteemed authors and illustrators, stories about favorite characters, fascinating nonfiction, and more!

This book is perfect for a **Progressing Reader** who:
• can figure out unknown words by using picture and context clues;
• can recognize beginning, middle, and ending sounds;
• can make and confirm predictions about what will happen in the text; and
• can distinguish between fiction and nonfiction.

Here are some **activities** you can do during and after reading this book:
• Make Connections: The Berrykins are excited for show-and-tell because they will get to share special things with their friends. Have you ever brought something to school for show-and-tell? What did you bring?
• Sight Words: Sight words are frequently used words that readers know just by looking at them. Knowing these words helps children become efficient and smooth readers. The words listed below are sight words used in this book. As you are reading or rereading the story, have the child point out the sight words.

blue	her	take
find	is	the
help	make	to

Remember, sharing the love of reading with a child is the best gift you can give!

—Bonnie Bader, EdM
 Penguin Young Readers program

*Penguin Young Readers are leveled by independent reviewers applying the standards developed by Irene Fountas and Gay Su Pinnell in *Matching Books to Readers: Using Leveled Books in Guided Reading*, Heinemann, 1999.

Penguin Young Readers
Published by the Penguin Group
Penguin Group (USA) Inc., 375 Hudson Street, New York, New York 10014, USA
Penguin Group (Canada), 90 Eglinton Avenue East, Suite 700, Toronto, Ontario M4P 2Y3, Canada
(a division of Pearson Penguin Canada Inc.)
Penguin Books Ltd, 80 Strand, London WC2R 0RL, England
Penguin Ireland, 25 St Stephen's Green, Dublin 2, Ireland (a division of Penguin Books Ltd)
Penguin Group (Australia), 707 Collins Street, Melbourne, Victoria 3008, Australia
(a division of Pearson Australia Group Pty Ltd)
Penguin Books India Pvt Ltd, 11 Community Centre, Panchsheel Park, New Delhi—110 017, India
Penguin Group (NZ), 67 Apollo Drive, Rosedale, Auckland 0632, New Zealand
(a division of Pearson New Zealand Ltd)
Penguin Books (South Africa), Rosebank Office Park, 181 Jan Smuts Avenue,
Parktown North 2193, South Africa
Penguin China, B7 Jiaming Center, 27 East Third Ring Road North,
Chaoyang District, Beijing 100020, China

Penguin Books Ltd., Registered Offices: 80 Strand, London WC2R 0RL, England

Strawberry Shortcake™ and related trademarks © 2013 Those Characters From Cleveland, Inc.
Used under license by Penguin Young Readers Group. All rights reserved. Published by Penguin Young
Readers, an imprint of Penguin Group (USA) Inc., 345 Hudson Street, New York, New York 10014.
Manufactured in China.

ISBN 978-0-448-46475-6   10 9 8 7 6 5 4 3 2 1

Show-and-Tell

by Lana Jacobs
illustrated by MJ Illustrations

Penguin Young Readers
An Imprint of Penguin Group (USA) Inc.

The Berrykins are excited.

Tomorrow is Show-and-Tell Day

at school!

Everyone will bring something
special to share with the class.

Berrykin Blue will bring
her favorite toy.

Berrykin Bubbles will bring
her favorite bracelet.

Oh no!

Berrykin Belle does not know
what to bring.

Berrykin Belle knows what to do.

She will ask her friends for help.

Berrykin Belle visits

Lemon Meringue at her salon.

Lemon offers Belle a bow.

It makes her look berry pretty.

No, that is not right

for Berrykin Belle.

Berrykin Belle visits Blueberry

Muffin at her bookstore.

How about a book?

Everyone loves to read books.

No, that is not right

for Berrykin Belle.

Berrykin Belle visits

Orange Blossom at her shop.

Orange holds out a pair

of sunglasses.

The Berrykins can take turns
trying on the sunglasses
during show-and-tell.
No, that is not right
for Berrykin Belle.

Berrykin Belle is

running out of time.

Will she ever find something

to bring to show-and-tell?

Here comes

Strawberry Shortcake.

Maybe she will have an idea!

Strawberry knows what to do.

Berrykin Belle should not borrow something from a friend.

She should make something.

Berrykin Belle will make

a book about her friends.

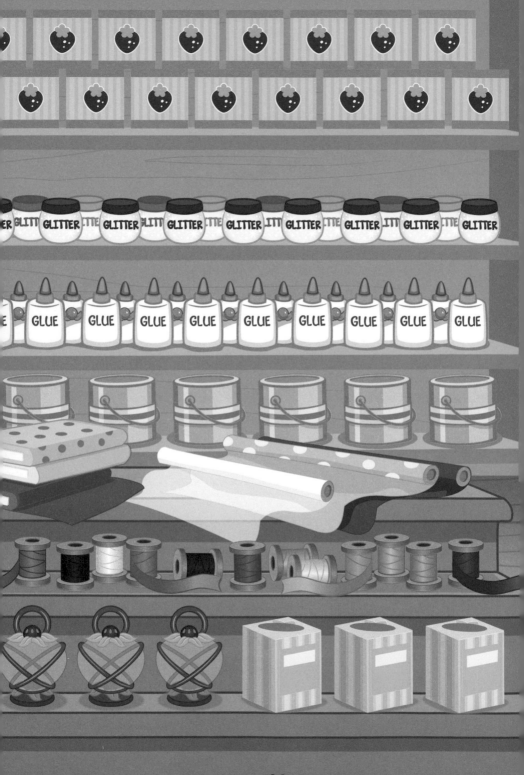

Berrykin Belle and Strawberry

go shopping.

At home, they find pictures.

Then Strawberry gets the scissors.

And Berrykin Belle gets the tape.

Berrykin Belle makes a
scrapbook about her friends.
The book will show
everything her friends
do for her.

They take her on berry fun picnics

to Berry Bitty Grove.

Plum Pudding teaches

her how to dance.

Strawberry gives the best hugs.

The scrapbook is ready

for show-and-tell!

The Berrykins look

at the pictures.

Here is Blueberry

reading to Berrykin Belle.

There is Lemon painting

Berrykin Belle's nails.

Look!

Here are the stars

of the scrapbook.

They came to visit Berrykin Belle.

She is berry lucky

to have such great friends!